THE KING'S DECREE

BY

TORINA KINGSLEY

A Wild Ink Publishing Publishing Original
wild-ink-publishing.com

Copyright © 2024 Torina Kingsley
Edited by Brittany McMunn
Layout & Design: Abigail Wild

ISBN: 978-1-958531-91-4

To anyone who has ever felt like they don't belong—
you do!

I

DEVINA

Once upon a time, there lived a princess named Devina. Well... maybe "lived" wasn't the best term. She wasn't a zombie or some undead creature roaming the countryside, though she often thought it'd be easier than what she was: just a girl. Just me.

I tore my gaze from the mirror before me, silencing my internal monologue as I did. Once, I cherished time in front of it, twisting and twirling in every dress I could get my hands on. Jades, royal blues, and scarletts so deep, they were almost purple highlighted hazel eyes that rivaled my mother's. Her laughter echoes in my memories, distant like a dream, as does my own. But that was before.

With a heavy sigh, I flopped onto the bed, not caring that I looked nearly as disheveled as I felt inside. Exactly a year ago, the curse struck me like a bolt of lightning on a sunny day. That's what it felt like, anyway. An invisible parasite latched on, sapping all my emotions, not just the happy ones. I became a shell of a person. Nothing more than a husk where a princess once stood.

I wish I knew what happened to make me feel this way. I wonder, sometimes, if I did something wrong and I am being punished. I also wonder if I didn't do anything to deserve this; maybe Fate simply dealt me a cruel hand. Mostly, I wonder if anyone else feels this way. Does anyone else understand how it feels to feel... nothing?

Now, on the eve of my sixteenth birthday, I lie on my bed, staring at the intricate tapestries adorning the walls. By now, I've memorized every pattern and swirl, every symbol and satyr. Nothing is new to me. That's how life feels, too—like I've seen already it all and have tired of it.

A sharp knock sounds on my bed chamber door, but I'm not surprised. Tomorrow, I'll be the center of attention and I'm certain my parents have expectations. What I should wear, what I should say, how I should act. *How I should feel.*

"Yes?" I croak, my own voice unfamiliar to my ears. When is the last time I spoke?

"It's Esme, Your Highness!"

I sigh, knowing what's coming.

"Come in," I call reluctantly.

My father's cheerful attendant flings open the door and springs inside. In a few strides, she crosses to the window and rips open the curtains, much to my displeasure. Rays of sunlight stream into my room, searing my eyes as they struggle to adjust.

"How about a stroll through the gardens before bed, Your Highness? Time outside would do you some good." She flashes a smile almost as bright as the still-stinging sunlight.

I resist a groan. I know she means well, and I certainly can't blame her for doing her job.

"To what do I owe the pleasure of your visit, Esme?" I ask, dramatically sliding off the bed to my feet. I'm sure the motion didn't look graceful, but Esme just looks happy I made any effort at all.

She drops into a curtsy, the voluminous folds of her skirts pooling like water. "You have been summoned," she says without meeting my eyes, "by His Majesty."

That's certainly a surprise. Or perhaps not. I haven't spoken to my father in weeks, but not for lack of trying on his part. By now, I'm sure he's frustrated with my behavior over the past year. An official summons used to mean donning one of my many fine dresses, freshly plaited hair, and accessories to match. Today, I look down at my plain gown, my long, loose hair, and say, "Then please take me to him."

Esme hesitates but, thankfully, decides against it. She swallows hard and plasters another smile on her face. With a nod, she moves to the door and I fall in step behind her. The hallway air feels strange on my skin, light compared to the staleness of my self-made dungeon. The rest of the castle buzzes with life and activity. Courtiers, nobles, and visitors dart around the corridors like schools of brightly colored fish. Sunlight streams through the narrow windows onto the rich, wine-colored rugs.

Among all this light and color, I feel particularly out of place in my cream gown, like a white flag marching toward surrender. Still, I nod politely in acknowledgment to those I pass, though I can't bring myself to return their smiles.

We reach the grand, gilded, double doors to the throne room. The two guards on either side opened them and announced our presence: "Princess Devina, Your Majesty."

The whole castle is glorious, but the throne room truly shines. The white marble floor reflects the sunlight, or at night, the glow of candles from chandeliers and candelabra. A plum rug flecked with golden stars runs the length of the room, up to the huge golden thrones where my parents sit side by side, their hands clasped. My mother's smile is tender, gentle, and genuine, much like her. I tell my lips to smile back, but they don't. I wonder if they still know how.

"Your Majesties," I murmur, dipping into a curtsy.

"Oh, do get up, sweetheart," my mother tuts, her hazel eyes glimmering. In fact, she and my father both appear more pleased to see me than usual.

"My darling, Devina!" my father's voice booms, easily filling the room. Rising from his seat, he crosses over to me. He holds me at arm's length, surveying me. "You look well." But his eyes give him away.

"You don't have to lie," I whisper.

"No, truly, you do!" He kisses me on the cheek, his long beard scratchy against my face, and I almost feel a flicker of something—warmth? Then, just as quickly, it is gone.

"Thank you, Father." A sudden wave of self-consciousness crashes over me. I awkwardly smooth the front of my skirts with my hands, now wishing I had washed and dressed.

"I'm sure you're wondering why we've summoned you," my father's voice echoes in the otherwise empty throne room.

I nod silently.

"We have exciting news," my mother says. She grins wider, but mine sinks. My heartbeat thunders in my chest, only emphasized by the thoughts stumbling out of control

What good am I to my people if I can't take care of myself? What good am I to my country? What good am I if...

What good am I?

My father nods in agreement and for a moment, I think he can hear my thoughts. "Our dear Devina," he says, smiling at me again. They're doing an awful lot of smiling. "For the past year, you have been battling with a terrible ailment. I cannot begin to imagine how you've felt."

He makes it sound like I'm fighting. Like I'm trying.

"Your mother and I feel nearly powerless to assist you."

I look down at my feet. I can't help but feel guilty. Surely, it's selfish to be so fortunate in life and yet not feel any joy in it.

"That is why, our dear Devina," my father continues, "we have hatched a plan."

"We've tried every doctor—"

"Tomorrow, to celebrate your sixteenth birthday, we will issue a decree: Anyone who is able to make you smile will win your hand in marriage!"

For a moment, I think he's joking, but then I remember whose mouth the words poured from.

"M-marriage?" I stammer. "You want me to be married?"

"No, darling," my mother's voice is sweet like the spoonful of honey before the medicine. "We want you to be *happy*. Surely anyone who is able to make you smile should be your life partner. And they will be rewarded by becoming heir to the throne."

Heir to the... what does that make me?

The voices around me garble, muffled as if I'm underwater rather than drowning in my own thoughts. The pressure builds, my breath quickening as the realization of what they've decided sets in.

A wife. I would be someone's wife.

I can hardly function on a daily basis, and they want me to be someone's wife? I can scarcely summon any kind of emotion, and they expect someone to make me laugh?

This plan is obviously one born from desperation; they're running out of ideas.

"I... I..." The words don't come. I feel like I'm trapped in a nightmare where I scream but there is no sound.

My mother's eyes swim with concern. "We know how it sounds, sweetheart, but give it a chance."

"We are confident a prince will be able to bring joy to your heart once again."

For the first time in a long while, my emotions take over. Rage flares, my cheeks burning red, "I don't want some prince to make me happy!"

My father's expression darkens like the calm before the storm. My mother turns away, her smile falling.

"It will be announced tomorrow, no matter your thoughts on the subject," my father spits through gritted teeth. "You may return to your chambers."

"But—"

"*Now*, Devina."

I suck in a breath and obey, neither out of habit nor respect for my king, but out of desire to be left alone. Or better yet, forgotten.

But I was born with a title before my name, and will therefore be thrust into the spotlight my whole life. *And tomorrow...*

Dread settles like a heavy blanket around my shoulders, increasing with each reluctant step. Esme leads the way, more as a formality. I could walk these halls with my eyes shut tight and not get lost, but a princess never walks alone. Curious eyes lock on me as I pass, the questions behind them burning, searing. But I can't meet their gaze.

We finally reach my chambers and relief washes over me at the sight of my sanctuary.

"Rest well, Your Highness," Esme says, her voice full of tenderness.

I silently nod and close the door behind her, sinking onto the floor and dissolving into tears.

Happy birthday to me.

2

YASMIN

"Yasmin! Tell us a story!"

Little Orla tugs at the hem of my skirt, her round face shining up at me like the moon. She's always the most eager for my stories.

"Oh, I wish I had time," I pat her on the head and smile, "but my father is expecting me back home."

"Just a short one, then!" One of the other children yells.

In moments, I'm surrounded by kids clamoring, poking me in the ribs, tugging at my clothes. I laugh helplessly, completely at their mercy. I remember when I was younger and bothered the older kids to play with me, too. It's strange, now, to be the elder of the group. I'm almost sixteen, after all—practically ancient.

"Okay, fine," I laugh, throwing my hands up in defeat. "A short one. Everyone sit."

Like obedient dogs, the kids plop onto their bottoms, staring up at me expectantly.

"Once upon a time…" I begin, but little Orla shakes her head, her bottom lip pouting stubbornly.

"They always start like that!" she whines. "Do something different!"

I think for a moment, my finger tapping my temples. Then, I thrust my finger into the air. "Aha!" I yell. "I've got it!"

Seven pairs of eyes widen.

"*Twice* upon a time!"

"Boooo!"

I shrug dramatically with a mischievous grin. What can I say? I love an audience.

"Stay with me, now," I say, holding my hands out. "*Twice* upon a time, there lived twin sisters, Ayla and Beela. They did everything together and were nearly impossible to tell apart. One day, Ayla and Beela walked to the well to gather some water. Little did they know…" I pause and lower my voice. The kids learn forward, willing me with their glances to continue. "A wolf was waiting for a tasty snack!"

My audience gasps as I pause for emphasis.

"The wolf leaped at Ayla, hoping to take a bite. Ayla rolled out of the way, quick as a cat. Then, Beela ran up and stood behind the wolf. 'Come and get me!' she cried."

Orla shifts where she sits, the tension getting to her.

"The wolf snarled and jumped at Beela who darted out of the way and hid behind the well." I hunch a little, my movements mimicking the canine from my tale. "The wolf stalked toward the well to get her… then whirled around to see the same girl!

Confused and scared, the wolf turned back toward the well—to see the smiling girl standing there, too. Back and forth, back and forth, the wolf howled in confusion. The sisters took the chance to scoop the wolf up and drop him into the well."

Victorious cheers erupted, their claps punctuating my character's victory.

"Ayla and Beela were heroes, and they didn't even mind when their parents congratulated them... and mixed up their names. Just another day for the twins!"

"Hooray!" My audience claps crescendo, and I take a low bow with a flourish.

"And now, I must fly!" I say before anyone can complain, and take off at a sprint. The rolling hills are no match for my adrenaline, the rush as I run fueling each stride. The branching dirt paths tempt me, each promising their own adventure, but my father would be waiting and I was already late. Again.

All around, people laugh and shout, haggle and yell, flirt and finagle. Most of them acknowledge me with a wave which I return as I keep running. I love each voice, brick, and blade of grass as wholly as I love my home.

Still, a part of me wonders if I'll ever see anywhere else...

My daydreams are cut short as my front door comes into view. True to form, he's sitting beside the hearth as I step inside.

"Yasmin!" he exclaims, rising slowly to his feet. "Didn't I expect you home half an hour ago?"

I smile sheepishly. "I'm sorry, Father. The children wanted me to tell them a story."

"Is that all you do—tell stories?" To anyone else, his tone might have sounded surly. But I knew better. A smirk tugged at his lips, but only just. My mother used to tell stories, too.

"Not all," I reply. "Sometimes I tell jokes, too."

My father barks a laugh, his smile cracking wide like a dam bursting open.

"Fine, fine," he says, catching his breath. Suddenly, his laughter turns to wheezing as a hacking fit takes hold of him. A pit forms in my stomach and I hasten to fetch water. He accepts it with trembling hands, but soon, the fit subsides and with it, the knot in my gut.

He looks at me with foggy, old eyes. "It's getting harder for me to work, my child. I'm growing too old for the fields."

And in a moment, the knot is back. I suck in a breath, realizing where this is going. Maybe if I beat him to the punch, it won't sting as badly.

"I can work the fields in your stead."

He snorts. "You? You wouldn't last a day out there, my dear. No, not the fields. But I do want to put you to work." He takes a slow sip with steadier hands. "You'll do well in the castle kitchens."

My heart leaps. The castle? Towering over us from the North, its presence a humbling reminder of our place in the world. As a child, I dreamed of its walls coming to life, a gargantuan creature stomping around the countryside. Even from afar, rumors sparked imaginations. Our village often prattled on about what the king proclaimed, what the queen must wear, and what meals they must be served. I've always wanted to know the truth for myself.

Then, my heart sinks like a stone in a well. Working in the castle means leaving home, leaving him. *And my freedom.* The thought pricks, but I don't dare voice it. Voicing fears gives them power. At least, that's what mother used to say.

I lick my suddenly dry lips. "Are you sure, Father?" I ask. "Perhaps there's something else I could—"

He shakes his head solemnly. "It's already been settled, Yasmin. You will begin tomorrow at dawn."

I frown. "And I don't get a say in this?"

My father sighs. "You will get most of your meals at the castle and bring home more money for us than I can." He hesitates, a visible lump rising in his throat. "Please, Yasmin. I need your help."

I look at my father, really look at him. His gnarled hands flecked with calluses and sunspots, bowed back, and tired eyes. Scars he carries to survive. Pain he endures for me. "Of course, I will help."

He visibly relaxes. "Thank you."

The air between us feels heavy with guilt. My prideful father's for asking my help and mine for being so blind. I obediently help him make some stew on the hearth. While I'm stirring the pot, my mind begins to wander.

What will the castle be like? Who will I meet? I know the princess is around my age; I wonder if I will see her. I've heard she is beautiful and kind, but sad.

I sprinkle some herbs into the stew. Working in the kitchen, it's unlikely I'll ever meet the princess. But maybe I'll make some other friends there. And maybe I'll get more than one hot meal a day.

Maybe this won't be so bad, after all.

3

DEVINA

Get up, Devina, I tell myself. *It's time to get up.*

I don't move.

How long have I been in bed? It's hard to tell. I still have the curtains drawn so I can't judge the passage of time by the sun. Has it been four hours, five hours, eight hours? I have no idea.

My back aches in protest, but it does little to motivate me out of bed. Instead, I roll onto my side so I can survey a new corner of the room rather than tapestries. My wardrobe seems to stare back, and I'm suddenly hyper-aware of the sweat causing my nightgown to cling. I would be embarrassed if I were able to access that emotion, but it's far away, as if on the very bottom of a riverbed. All I feel is a pale indifference.

I'm sure I'll be washed before the princes' arrive.

Esme will undoubtedly skip through my doors, armed with a sponge and sweet-smelling soaps. I'll be dressed in one of my finest gowns, like a doll, and presented to whoever deigns to try and make me smile. Since the prize for success is my hand in marriage and the future throne, I'm sure there will be many.

A new, terrible thought suddenly strikes me. What if my condition is contagious? What if everyone who comes through the doors in hopes of curing me leaves with the same ailment? What if...

The worries swarm like bees, buzzing around in my head until they drown out everything else. My breath catches in my throat as the panic sets in.

I bury my head under the blankets, listening to my shallow, shaky breaths in my cocoon. In. Out. In. Out. It's all I can do to calm the buzz of my thoughts, the racing of my heart. Loud raps on my door startle me, threatening to undo the little progress I made quelling my episode.

"Happy birthday, Your Highness! It's time to get ready for your first round of visitors!"

First round? There are rounds?

I throw a pillow over my face in response. "No, thank you," I mutter, only half caring whether or not I can be understood through the pillow.

Esme enters anyway. "It's a beautiful day, Princess!" She trills like an overenthusiastic bird. I uncover my face and watch warily as she goes to my wardrobe and flings the doors wide. "Which gown would you like to wear?"

I let out a sigh. "I don't care," I say, truthfully.

Esme tuts. "Nonsense! Do come and select one, Your Highness, or I'll be forced to put you in the pink frilly one you *so* adore..."

"I'm up, I'm up!" I spring out of bed. There are a few sights I loathe more than myself in that frilly, pink dress.

After some time, I am bathed, washed, combed, and perfumed, smelling of vanilla and lilacs. If I'm honest, it feels good to be clean. I select a pale blue gown and silver slippers to match how I feel: light. The difference feels strange to me, just as the fresh air did the day prior. I take a seat at my vanity, shifting so Esme can begin styling my hair. Her hands are careful, gentle braiding and pinning my thick curls into place. When she's done, I turn to face the mirror.

"Oh, Your Highness. You look enchanting!" Esme cries, pleased with herself.

I stare at myself in the looking glass. Sad, brown eyes gaze back at me, poorly masked by silk and a silver circlet crowning my head. I certainly look the part.

"Have you eaten anything today, Your Highness?" Esme asks. "You'll need plenty of energy." She lowers her voice slightly, concern bleeding into her tone. "It's going to be a long day."

My heart sinks at her implication. I shake my head. I barely remember to eat anymore.

"I'll get you something," Esme says.

"Actually, may I go to the kitchens myself?"

Esme narrows her eyes, studying me. "But you're the princess."

I shrug. "It's my birthday." Truthfully, I'm trying to stall. The sooner I arrive at the throne room, the sooner I'll have to deal with strangers.

Esme's lips curl, but she knows better than to argue. "Very well," she says. "But take care not to dawdle."

I dawdle as much as I can.

The kitchens are at the South end of the castle, and it should only take me a few minutes to get there. Today it takes me fifteen. I look out the windows, admire paintings and tapestries, and stare at stalwart suits of armor. I examine the stone walls, searching for imperfections. I invent stories in my head about where a passerby may be going or why.

When I was little, the castle felt infinite, all labyrinthine twists and turns and endless hallways. It feels significantly smaller, now. I know all its secrets.

When I arrive at the kitchens, the kindly head cook pulls me into an embrace. "I haven't seen you in so long, Your Highness!" she gushes, dipping into a formal bow. "Your cake is prepared for later, but I can whip you up a special birthday treat now—"

I hold up a hand. "Not necessary, Maeta. Can I just have some soup and bread, please?"

She raises an eyebrow. "That's all? For a birthday feast? I won't have it! Sit down, Your Highness, and let me make you something extravagant."

I could argue, but Maeta is a welcome change of pace.

She and about five or six familiar faces, get to work. I sit at a counter, sipping water and watching them whirl around the kitchen. One in particular catches my eye. A lanky girl about my age stands frozen, uncertainty painted across her freckled face. Maeta whispers to her, pointing out where tools and ingredients are located. Our eyes meet as she crosses the room and sinks into a deep, clumsy curtsey.

"Your Highness."

I motion for her to rise.

"Happy birthday! You're sixteen today, yes?"

I nod, taken aback by her casual tone. Her voice is bubbly, and captivating, unlike the stiff way most speak to me

"I turned sixteen a few months ago," she says, her voice flitting like birdsong. "I feel *ancient*. Soon we'll need canes and wonder where all our teeth are!"

"I think I still have all of mine," I offer.

The girl grins. "Give it another year."

"Yasmin!" Maeta hisses under her breath. "That is no way to speak to our princess." Her face flushes red, but she plasters on a mask of composure. "Back to work, darling. Her Highness surely can't stay here all day."

I would if I could, I think. The girl—Yasmin—catches my eye again, winks, and turns away. Then, I'm lost in the fabulous aromas swirling throughout the room. I close my eyes and let the sounds and smells wash over me. Warm vanilla fills my lungs, complimented by the clinks of spoons stirring, the crackle of eggshells, and the roar of a fire being tended, like a sweet symphony of sounds.

"Your Highness!"

I recognize Esme's voice before I see her. I cringe, squeezing my eyes tighter.

"Your Highness, it's past time for you to be in the throne room. The first guest has arrived!"

"Esme, let the girl eat," Maeta sets the fruits of her labor in front of me: a tower of teacakes, fried eggs, and a mug of steaming cocoa. My mouth waters.

"His Majesty is waiting," Esme says, wringing her hands.

I ignore her, sinking my teeth into a teacake. Nutty hints and the tang of currants dance on my taste buds. *When is the last time I had a warm meal?* Most nights, my meals grow cold on a tray outside my door. I shovel more into my mouth, neglecting all etiquette.

Esme studies me a moment, her eyes soften. "Eat with haste, Your Highness," she says. I suspect her thoughts mirror mine.

"Do you like it?" Yasmin is back, wiping her hands on a towel. Her grin is a little lopsided, lending her a permanently mischievous expression. She almost glows with a natural zest for life.

I used to be like that.

"It's delicious," I say truthfully.

"Made it *all* myself," she beams. "First day in the kitchens, too. Who knew I was a culinary genius?" She flourishes her comment with a dramatic bow. Maeta is distracted and I almost giggle when I imagine her reaction to Yasmin's theatrics.

I like her, I decide.

I open my mouth to ask her a question, but Esme interjects.

"We must go, Your Highness!"

I reluctantly push away my plate. "Thank you," I say with as much earnestness as I can muster. "I didn't realize I needed that."

"Come back whenever you need to, Your Highness," Maeta says. She slips a square of cloth into my hands. "You're always welcome here." From the knot at the top, I suspect there are sweets inside.

"I hope to see you again, Your Highness." Yasmin aims her crooked grin at me.

"I hope so, too," I reply. To my surprise, I mean it. I haven't looked forward to seeing anyone for a long time.

Esme takes my hand and nearly drags me out the door. We march down the corridors without a word. My heart flutters like a caged bird against my ribs. The realization hits me hard: I'm nervous.

Who will I meet? What will I say?

We stop outside the doors to the throne room. With a gentle, almost maternal touch, Esme smooths my hair from my brow and straightens my circlet. "I pray there is someone who can bring you a job, Your Highness," she murmurs.

I give her a grateful look. "Thank you," I say.

Esme raps on the door with her knuckles until we're permitted to enter.

I square my shoulders, lift my chin, and enter the throne room to meet my future husband.

4

YASMIN

Working in the kitchens isn't so bad, I think.

But then, it's time for dinner. The kitchens fill with noise and sound, heat and sweat, bodies in motion, and booming voices. Three days of this isn't enough to adjust to the constant hustle and bustle. Fatigue wears me like a garment, one I can't seem to shed.

I arrive at the castle before sunrise and don't leave until sundown. I've been told I'll work six days a week, with the seventh for much-needed rest. I already miss my friends and my father but confident I'm making a difference. Perhaps in more ways than one.

Tonight is even more of an affair than usual. One of the visiting princes has been asked to stay for dinner, which means more food than usual and of even more extravagant quality. Among the whirl and swirl of the kitchen are quail eggs, potatoes, large slabs of meat, several different soups, a variety of cheeses, fish, and vividly hued fruit. My eyes grow round as dinner plates at the sight. Are they really going to eat all of that?

"Yasmin!" Maeta shouts above the din of pots and plates clattering. "I need you to go to the cellar."

I perform an elaborate salute. "Yes, ma'am!" I reply.

"Don't mock me, girl," she says, swatting gently at my arm. "We need more flour and salted butter. Do you know where you're going?"

"I-I didn't mean..." Maeta has been nothing but kind to me, and I appreciate her gentle guidance. Somehow, she is both tender and tough, always willing to offer praise but also unafraid to keep the staff in line. "I think so," I say. I followed someone to the cellar last night, after all. The castle is like a maze, but I've always had a good sense of direction.

"Don't dilly-dally," Maeta says, and I respond with a wave as I dash out of the kitchens.

The halls are as beautiful as anything else in the castle. Silk tapestries of battles and warriors line the walls, each more intricate than the last. I imagine the weary hands that crafted them, not unlike my own.

I turn down one corridor after another until I realize my mistake.

I definitely came from there, I think, chewing on my bottom lip. Perhaps my sense of direction isn't as good as I thought. I pick a direction and follow it, the soft padding of my steps now feels loud in the stillness. I don't recognize this part of the castle. The lighting is poor and more cavernous. The rugs on the floor are ragged, and the stone walls are unadorned. Few people must come here.

It's why I'm shocked at the sound of sniffles and sobs.

I whirl around, my pulse beating rapidly. "Who's there?" No reply comes, but tension hangs in the air like the cal, before a storm.

It's just a rat, I tell myself. I have no reason to be afraid. Still, being lost and alone in an unknown place would make anyone nervous.

I shake my head, roll my shoulders, and prepare to walk back down the corridor.

"Yasmin?"

My spine stiffens at the sound of my own name, then relaxes. Someone from the kitchen must have come looking for me. I hope once I explain what happened, I won't be in too much trouble.

"Don't tell Maeta I got lost," I beg as I turn around. "I want her to think I'm—"

The princess back stares at me, tears running down her round face.

Well. This is unexpected.

At first, I freeze in surprise at the sight of the princess, but then I register she's crying. Instinctively, I move to embrace her, but then I stop myself. It wouldn't be appropriate for the new kitchen girl to hug the princess.

"Are you—alright, Your Highness?" I ask instead, bringing my arms awkwardly back to my sides.

"Devina," she whispers. "Call me Devina."

"Um, okay," I say, smiling reassuringly at her. "Devina it is Your Highness. I mean..." I roll my eyes at myself. "Devina. Right."

The princess—Devina—nods. Her arms are wrapped around her as if protecting herself from an unknown attacker. Tears still roll down her face, but she wipes them impatiently away with the back of her hand. She's dressed just as beautifully as she was two days ago but in a green gown today instead of blue. I wonder what it's like to have more than one dress.

"What are you doing down here?"

She sniffles, burying her face in her knees. "Hiding," she says, her voice muffled by the fabric.

I sink to the floor beside her, her shoulder brushing against mine. "From who?"

"From everyone."

"Hm. Does that include me? Do you want me to leave?" I ask, omitting the fact I have no idea where I am.

She hesitates, then shakes her head. "Please don't," she says. Then, she sits on the moth-eaten carpet, hugging her knees to her chest. After a moment, I sit beside her. I'm definitely going to be in trouble when I return to the kitchens, but I push the thought out of my head.

I wonder what's wrong, and, most of all, how to ask. *How does one comfort royalty?* I'm tempted to just ask—to blurt out the first thing that pops into my head but the last thing I need is to upset the princess further. My father depends on me. I need this job.

Her voice interrupts the silence before I get the chance. "What are *you* doing down here?"

My cheeks burn. "I was on my way to the cellar," I confess, "but I got lost. Not my finest moment."

"You're not too far," she says. "I can take you there." She wipes at her face with a silken sleeve.

"That's not—"

"I'm fine." Her voice is firm, steady. I don't dare to push further.

"Thank you, Pr-uh, Devina," I say. I grin at her and watch her lips quiver as if trying to return the gesture. In the end, she just nods.

We sit in silence for several minutes. Outwardly, I pick at the loose threads in my cotton apron, a stark contrast to Devina's emerald pleats and gold embroidery. Inwardly, my mind gallops like a racehorse. I don't know how to make conversation with a weeping princess. My stomach twists with concern and something else. Unease but also... curiousity? Fondness? I can't quite put my finger on it. It reminds me of the feeling before rolling down a steep hill or diving off a ledge into the lake on a hot summer day. The mixture of fear and excitement overwhelms everything else. I'm so consumed with my thoughts, I nearly forget to speak. Oddly enough, the silence between us doesn't feel awkward. In fact, it feels comfortable, familiar.

She sniffles, blinks away further tears, and looks sideways at me. "Thank you," she says.

"For what?"

"Simply sitting with me. Just being here."

"You're welcome," I say. I picture her days, endlessly presented to strangers more interested in the prize that comes with bringing her joy than her. "When my mother passed away, I hated when people tried to cheer me up. I just wanted to be sad for a while, in silence."

She nods and rolls her eyes. "I imagine about my father's... arrangement?"

I wince. "I imagine it's not going particularly well?"

Her silence speaks volumes. Devina stands and brushes the dirt off her skirts then helps me to my feet. "The cellar is this way." She heads in the opposite direction I was going.

Oops. I follow, relieved.

"I've heard the same joke at least five times now," she continues. "You know the one about the rabbit and the snake?"

I snort. "Of course, I do. It wasn't funny the first time."

"Exactly!" she says.

"What else do they try?"

The princess shakes her head. "Everything. Jokes, singing, stories, silly voices, funny faces. The prince who's here today brought *puppets* and threatened to bring them to dinner, too. That's when I ran and hid."

I shudder. I wouldn't want to eat dinner with puppets, either.

"Do you think any of them will succeed?"

Do you want them to? The question claws at my throat but I stifle it.

She grows quiet and I don't push the subject. We amble in silence until our surroundings begin to look vaguely familiar, and finally, we arrive at the cellar. I quickly grab some flour and butter, hoping Maeta still needs them and didn't send someone else.

"Thanks for showing me the way," I shift my weight nervously. "And I'm sorry you're probably going to hear rabbit joke at least a thousand more times."

There it is—the tiniest flicker of a smile on her lips—distant and faint, like something I can see far beneath the surface of cloudy water. "I hope they come up with some better material."

"I hope so too, for your sanity."

"Can I walk with you back to the kitchens?"

I'm surprised she wants to. "Of course. Maybe Maeta won't be cross if she thinks you're to blame for my tardiness."

Terrifle jokes spill from our lips, one after another. My father has a few classics, and I tell them to the princess with gusto, she groans at each awful punchline making my stomach flutter. Devina tells me one that's so bad it's almost funny, and I'm still chuckling when I nearly stroll head-first into Maeta.

"What took you so long?" she cries as she snatches the butter and flour from my arms. Her eyes lock on Devina, and she softens, dipping into a deep curtsy. "Begging your pardon, Your Highness," she says. "I didn't realize she was with you."

"Yasmin has been a great help to me this evening," Devina says. "I very much appreciate her company, and I'm sure she's a wonderful addition to the kitchen staff."

I can't help it—I briefly take Devina's hand in mine and squeeze it, as if to say thank you.

To my surprise, she squeezes mine back before withdrawing. "I'd better get back," she says softly, hurrying off before I can say goodbye.

When I turn around, Maeta stares at me, shock plastered on her face. "What?" I ask.

Maeta tilts her head. "She almost looked... happy."

5

DEVINA

Every day, princes come to the castle.

Every day I turn them away.

I watch, stone-faced, as prince after prince jumps through hoops for my entertainment. Some, literally. At first, I tried to smile out of pity, but I couldn't even manage that. Now, I watch them with an icy expression that refuses to melt. My father may have proclaimed this prize to bring me joy, but I see it for what it truly is—humiliating, demeaning. My worth reduced to endlessly judging the performances of strangers, who don't see me as anything other than a means to an end. Of what I can give them: the throne.

No, they do not—*will not*—know me. How could they when I hardly know myself?

In a way, I feel bad for them. I know they're trying their best. I watch the hope dim from their eyes the longer they stay and the more outlandish their stories, jokes, and songs become. I can only imagine what they whisper behind my back or beyond the castle walls. I'm sure they call me names; I'm sure they go home and tell their friends I'm hopeless, heartless, or worse.

Maybe I am hopeless. I certainly feel heartless. There's just nothing that moves me anymore. I am a shell of what I once was, hollow like the emptiness that plagues me.

At first, I was dismissive of my parent's idea. After a week of this hell, I am almost desperate for one of them to succeed. At least then I would know I'm not broken, forever incapable of feelings. I would make my parents, and the rest of the kingdom, happy. I would re-inspire hope in our people. I would quell the rumors and whispers forever. Maybe I would be happy.

Instead, I feel worse than usual. I feel like a failure.

It's no surprise when today's prince arrives, I barely muster the energy to curtsy. My sleep has been tormented with nightmares, abstract as a watercolor painting, but still scary enough to haunt me. I wake up every day feeling more drained than when I went to sleep.

"Princess Devina, it is a joy to make your acquaintance," he says, flashing unnaturally white teeth.

I wish I could respond in kind, but I simply nod.

"And how do you plan to bring the princess joy?" My father booms.

I look back at him, on his throne, and realize my mother isn't beside him. My frown deepens. Where could she be? Has she tired of this, too?

"I will play her *music*!" The prince crows, as if he isn't the fourth person to try this approach.

As he strums his lute, singing something about a maiden fair; my mind won't stay still enough for me to listen. I wish I could hide back in the halls again, accompanied only by the scurry of rats and the drip-drop of water. *Or Yasmin.* The way her voice somehow adds color to the room. I remember, too, the soft touch of her hand, and the mischievous warmth of her dark eyes.

I wonder when I'll see her again.

The prince finishes his song, and I realize, belatedly, I should be applauding.

I clap politely. "Thank you for your efforts."

"Oh, but I have another eight songs prepared!" he replies.

I frown and bite back a sharp reply. I turn to the king beside me. "Father, may I be excused. I'm not feeling well." The lie comes easily, though I doubt he believes me.

"You should be ashamed of yourself," the prince snaps.

I wheel back around but my response dies on my lips.

"So many people are trying," his eyes flash with fury, "and you refuse to—no, you *choose* to be miserable. Our efforts are all a waste of time. You are selfish, Princess Devina, for feeling the way you do. I hope you know that."

His words land like physical blows, confirming my deepest fear. I am selfish, stubborn, difficult. Tears spring to my eyes, brimming like the sadness that plagues me. I lose sleep wondering if everyone hates me, worrying that everyone who tries to help secretly resents me.

Apparently, they do.

"I'm s-sorry." My voice breaks, barely a whisper.

"You are dismissed," my father waves a hand.

Without another word, the prince gathers his instrument and storms out the door.

I collapse to my knees, weeping, my face hidden in my hands. I can't bear to look at my father and only register his presence when I feel his hand on my shoulder.

"I don't believe him," my father says. "You shouldn't, either."

I raise my head; tears stream down my face. "But he's right," I sniffle, barely audible. "I *am* selfish."

Father shakes his head, his eyes soft. "I don't understand what's wrong, I'll admit, but I do know you are a kind and gentle soul. You would never feel this way on purpose. We just haven't found the right person, or the right solution, yet." He squeezes my shoulder. "Perhaps we should call the doctor again. It's been several months; maybe he has thought of another remedy."

My heart sinks at the thought of seeing yet another doctor. Poked and prodded, bitter concoctions, one even bled me with leeches.

"I know last time was frightening," Father acknowledges, seeing the look on my face. "But we have to keep trying. Shall we visit Boren?" He offers me his arm.

Quietly, I nod and accept it.

We walk in silence to the East wing of the castle, the shuffle of our attendants following closely behind. Everyone who passes us bows or curtsies, and I'm so exhausted, I just nod in recognition. The prince's words still sting like a bug bite, one I'm not able to scratch. Fresh waves of tears periodically flow into my eyes, but I refuse to let them fall.

I am not selfish, I say to myself. *I am doing my best, too.*

When we reach the court doctor's quarters, Boren is busy with another patient, so I sit on a hard wooden bench, dangling my feet. My father paces in the corridor, deep lines formed on his brow.

A few minutes pass before Boren comes out, and the angular-faced man looks paler than usual.

"Your Majesty," he says, bowing to my father, and then to me. "Your Highness. Did you come to see the Queen?"

I hollow pit forms in my stomach, like a void threatening to swallow me whole. I look to my father, thoughts thundering in my ears, but he doesn't meet my gaze. "She is still with you?"

Boren nods, his expression unreadable. "I know her symptoms were mild last evening, but she is still quite dizzy and nauseous. I don't feel comfortable sending her back to her chambers yet."

"Mother is sick? Why didn't you tell me?"

Father sighs, looking tired. "She didn't want to give you any cause for alarm or distract you, Devina. You need to focus on your own ailment, not on your mother's health."

"Of course, I need to focus on my mother's health!" I snap. I turn to Boren. "What's wrong with her?"

"I don't yet have an answer for you, Your Highness, but I'm doing everything in my power to find out."

My heart pounds as if I just ran the length of the castle. What if I've been so self-absorbed, I didn't notice my mother's symptoms? Or worse—what if she's sick and it's my fault? What if my curse somehow extended to her?

I can't be here any longer.

Before my father or Boren can react, I take off down the corridors, weaving my way back to my chambers. When I arrive at my room, I slam the door behind me, and fling myself onto my bed, weeping.

If something happens to my mother, I'll never be happy again.

6

YASMIN

"Yasmin? Why are you awake?"

My father peers at me suspiciously as I plait my hair into a long braid and slip my feet into sandals. He's sitting by the fire where he fell asleep in his favorite chair, as usual. I stoop to kiss him on the cheek.

"I'm going to the castle," I reply.

"But why? Today's your day off, isn't it?" he asks.

I can't resist a grin. "It is. The princess requested my presence."

"The—the princess?" My father gapes at me, and I can't help but giggle at his expression. "What does she want with you?"

I shrug. "I don't know exactly," I think of her sad eyes, the tremble of her lips, "but I suspect she wants a friend."

"But you? A peasant girl?"

"Hey!" I cry in mock offense. "I'm an amazing friend, thank you very much. Best of the best. A treat for peasants and princesses alike."

My father chuckles and pats my hand. "You're right, my dear. Just be sure not to bore her with one of your long-winded stories."

I stick my tongue out at him and the door clicks closed behind me. The sun beats down on me, a welcome companion on my long trek to the castle. My first week in the kitchens, the walk left my feet blistered and muscles aching. But before long, the blisters callused over and I found myself enjoying early morning dew and the quiet.

Devina has escaped to the kitchens a few times since I found her crying. Her mother, she tells me, has been sick for over a week now. While princes still visit, the number has dwindled. It seems many of them are becoming skeptical their efforts will reap any reward. Devina says she can't remember the last time she felt happy or hope she would ever smile again.

It makes my heart hurt.

So, Maeta serves her food, and I serve her stories, but most often I just provide a listening ear. The unseen burden she shoulders weighs her down like an anchor. And yet, she doesn't complain—not to me, at least. Mostly, she seems concerned about how her she affects the other people in her life.

"It doesn't bother me," I tell her as we walk through the palace gardens.

I have never seen so many colors in one place. It's as if a rainbow has shattered and sprinkled its colors all over the ground. I touch a huge petal from an orange flower and marvel at its velvety softness. I wish blossoms like this grew in the village.

Devina looks at me. "It doesn't?"

I shake my head. "I'm used to my father, who's just a crotchety old man. Not that you're a crotchety old man," I hasten to add as Devina arcs a brow. "Just... you seem sad, not mean or grumpy."

"Sometimes I *am* grumpy," Devina says. "And sometimes I'm mean. Sometimes being cruel or angry feels better than being sad all the time."

"Are you angry about your mother?" I ask.

She considers the question. "Yes," she says quietly. "I'm mad Boren doesn't know what's happening. I'm mad Father pretends everything is fine. I'm mad I feel so empty I can't do anything about it."

I nod in understanding. I pluck a rose from a bush, gently pinching the stem in a thornless spot between two fingers. "I was angry when my mother was sick, too. It felt like Fate was punishing her and I didn't know why."

Devina is quiet, then murmurs, "I'm worried Fate is punishing me, too."

She sits on a marble bench under a willow tree, its long tendrils draping around her like a curtain. I part some of the branches and tentatively sit beside her. She watches as I remove thorns from the stem until it's clean, smooth. "It wouldn't dare," I say. Then, I reach my hand up, and she doesn't recoil, as I tuck the rose behind Devina's ear.

"Sometimes, a flower just needs a little space. Room to be." *A little love,* I wanted to say.

A single tear slides down her cheek.

"I think..." The complexity of what I want to say is difficult to articulate, and I stare ahead of me with furrowed brows. "I think sometimes life is too much. Too much hurt. Too much pressure. Too many expectations." I shift to face her directly. "I don't think you're being punished or cursed. I don't believe you're sick or anything is wrong with you at all. I think you're a beautiful soul weighed down by the burdens thrust on you."

The princess looks at me for a long time. Her lips quiver, and without really meaning to, I touch my fingers lightly to the side of her face.

"It's okay," I say. "And if it isn't, I'll be here with you."

For a fraction of a second, her lips twitch in an almost smile, and it's like I'm watching the sun rise for the first time. Just as quickly, it's gone, but she looks more peaceful, more calm.

"Thank you, Yasmin," Devina says. "That means so much to me."

I flush. "It's the least I can do," I say. "I know you would do the same for me."

"You do?"

I nod.

She flings her arms around my neck, catching me off guard, the rose behind her ear as scented as perfume. I hesitate a moment, then pull her close. For a long time, we sit in each other's arms, safe within the larger embrace of the willow tree. Here, like this, together, I feel a warmth in my heart I've never experienced before, and I am grateful.

The princess finally pulls away, tears sparkling on the tips of her lashes. She blushes and wipes them away with the back of her hand.

"I haven't felt like a good person lately," she confesses. "A good daughter or a good princess, and definitely not a good friend. But I want to be all those things. And the fact you think—" Her eyes shimmer, and she takes a deep breath. "You're important to me."

My insides do a backflip. "A good friend doesn't have to be in a good mood," I say. "All that matters is you're there for each other. That you care about each other. That you love each other."

Heat suddenly rises to my face, and I worry I've gone too far. But the princess takes my hand in hers and squeezes it. "You're right," she says. "Thank you, Yasmin."

"You're welcome, Devina."

We stand from the bench. With an exaggerated flourish, I offer my arm to the princess, and she accepts it. For a while, we tour silently around the gardens, arm in arm. I feel as if something has changed, but I'm unable to name it. Whatever it is, I feel more comfortable with the princess than ever.

"Tell me about where you live," Devina says, surveying a small pond. A tiny frog leaps from a lilypad as we approach, diving into the water.

"The village?" I repeat. "What do you want to know?"

The princess shrugs. "Well, I… I haven't been there in a long time. I should be more knowledgeable of what it's like. Someday, I'll be Queen."

I consider the town I've called home for my entire life. "Things move slower there," I say, "There's always work to be done, of course, but evenings are filled with children's laughter, stargazing, or songs by roaring bonfires. It's a place where families have traditions and secrets, stories and games, friendships that transcend the ages. The people are kind and hard-working. Well, except for old Matten, who just bullies all the kids into doing his chores. One time, I remember…"

I launch into a story about Matten and how the children once smeared peanut butter on the back of his shoes, so the dogs followed him and nipped at his ankles. An astonishing sound comes from Devina's mouth: laughter.

It rings gently like a bell, the most musical, beautiful sound I've ever heard. I stare at her, shocked into stillness.

She giggles, her hand covering her mouth, struggling to catch her breath. "What?"

"You—laughed," I croak in disbelief.

She blinks, wiping away the tears with a smile. "Oh. I suppose I did."

We stare at each other, then burst into hysterics once more. I only stop when the realization washes over me. "Wait, so…"

"If I tell my father," Devina says, "You could… You would…"

"Your Highness," Esme pants, running towards us. Her expression is wild, eyes wide with urgency. "Your Highness, I need you to come with me."

"What's wrong?" Concern wrinkles Devina's brow.

Esme wrings her hands. "Your mother…" She begins, but that's all Devina needs to hear. She turns to me.

"I'm sorry," she whispers, "but I must go."

"Of course," I say. "I'll see you tomorrow?"

She nods, her thoughts already miles away.

Esme gives me a look as if just registering my presence, but then she and Devina are off toward the castle, leaving me alone in the gardens.

7

DEVINA

I should be worried about my mother. I *am* worried about my mother. But as Esme hastens me from the gardens to the doctor's ward, all I can think about is Yasmin's eyes.

In the sunlight, golden rings sparkled around her irises, flecks of dark green dancing with warm amber hues.

I'm uncertain how, but when she smiles, her eyes reflect the gesture. It makes me want to smile, too. Today felt like a delicious dream. Each step brings me closer to my mother and yet, my mind still wanders the gardens with Yasmin.

My laugh felt unfamiliar, like a tickle in my throat. Still, it felt good. For in that fraction of a moment, I didn't feel hopeless, or despondent, or numb. I felt normal.

You're a beautiful soul weighed down by the burdens thrust on you. Her voice echoes in my head. *A beautiful soul.*

I'm comforted even just by imagining her voice.

I felt alive.

"Your Highness, I've asked Boren to come speak with you."

Grim reality descends on me again. The doctor emerges from the ward and shuts the heavy wooden door behind him. Esme curtsies and retreats to a polite distance.

Boren looks exhausted. Dark purple shadows lay beneath his eyes, and his graying hair is disheveled.

"Is my mother okay?" I ask, impatient.

He hesitates, and I feel all the breath leave my body.

"She is for now," he says. "But her fever is getting worse and won't go down. I'm afraid there's little I can do except keep her comfortable, Your Highness."

I need to sit. I need to sleep. I need to scream. I need to run. A million different impulses pull me in different directions, and all I can do is stand, motionless.

I wish Yasmin were here. I wish I were anywhere else.

I must look like I'm about to swoon because Boren takes my arm and looks at me intently. "Your Highness, are you alright?"

I nod, battling my emotions to keep tears from welling. "Take me to her."

Several long beds are set up in the room, separated by white curtains. We walk past them and into a private room, meant only for members of the royal family. Flickering candles attempt to lend warmth, but the room is still small, dark, and musty.

My mother lies in the bed at the center of the room. My father sits in a chair beside her. They both look up when I enter and smile weakly at me.

"Devina," my mother's voice, soft and raspy. "Come, have a seat. Your father was just leaving."

Father nods and stands. "I have some things to discuss with you, Boren, if you have a moment."

"Of course, Your Majesty," says Boren.

I take my father's place in the chair and hold my mother's hand. It's colder and clammier than usual. Beyond that, she looks like herself. Maybe Boren is wrong, and everything is fine. Maybe everything is going to be okay.

"How are you doing?" my mother inquires.

"I think I should be asking that of you," I reply.

She manages a weak laugh. "Oh, I'm fit as a fiddle," she says, a frequent expression of hers. "I'm not in any pain, just very weak."

"You don't look weak," I squeeze her hand. "You look strong like you always do."

"You must be thinking of yourself, Devina."

I shake my head. "I'm not strong." My eyes sting, glistening.

"Of course, you are," Mother insists. She struggles to sit up in bed, and I sling my arm around her shoulders to help her get comfortable. "You have to be strong to feel the weight of the world so heavily and still continue to live in it. I'm proud of you."

Like a dam bursting, tears roll down my cheeks. I open my mouth to disagree, but Yasmin's voice in my head cuts me off.

A beautiful soul.

I almost smile, and my mother takes notice. "What are you thinking about?"

Heat rushes to my face, and I press my hands to my cheeks.. My mother's previously raised brow ascends higher.

"I've met a girl…"

For the next half-hour, at least, I tell my mother all about Yasmin. I try not to ramble about her smile or the way her eyes look in the sunlight; instead, I talk about her mischievous sense of humor, her stories, and her kindness.

"She's wonderful," I say when I realize I've been rambling for a long time. "I'm glad to have met her."

My mother smiles. "I'm glad you have, too. I only wish I could meet her as well."

"Y-you can," I say, staggering to my feet. "You have plenty of time to meet her. She works in the kitchens."

Mother shakes her head slowly. "I don't know how much time I have left," she says softly. "Devina, I need you to know how much I love you—"

"No!" I fling my arms out. "I—I can get Yasmin right now. She might still be in the gardens. Let me go find her. I'll be right back."

I bunch my skirts into my hands, and run out the door, past Boren and my father, back out into the corridor. Faster and faster, I sprint away from my mother's sickbed, from the grim confirmation she is unwell, from the knowledge she is sicker than she looks. All that matters to me right now is I find Yasmin.

I finally reach the gardens, gasping for breath. I cup my hands around my mouth. "Yasmin!" I look frantically around, too frantically, the beautiful colors of flowers all blurring together.

Suddenly, it all seems too much. The hues are too bright, the scents too strong. A peaceful atmosphere has turned sinister.

Panic grows in my chest, and suddenly I'm drowning in it. I claw at my throat, unable to find relief and collapse to my knees as I dissolve into helpless tears. Any semblance of control I had is gone.

Am I dying?

I continue to gasp for air. My entire body trembles like a leaf on a branch, and a cold sweat beads at my temples. I feel both too hot and too cold at once. Could I have caught my mother's fever so quickly?

Finally, it begins to pass, and I can breathe again. I gasp for air as if my head has broken the water's surface. I hug myself tightly, imagining the arms around me are my mother's, or Yasmin's, bringing me comfort and stillness. I've never experienced anything like this before. Instead of feeling nothing, as I do normally, it's as if I felt everything at once.

"Devina?"

For a moment, I hope Yasmin has found me, but the voice is deep and masculine—my father's.

"Are you alright?" He gathers me into his arms, and I collapse against his chest.

"I think so," I say. I turn my face up to look at him and see that, for the first time in my lifetime, my father is crying.

"Father?" I croak from my suddenly bone-dry mouth. "Is it... Is it Mother?"

His eyes confirm my worst fear.

8

YASMIN

When a member of the royal family passes away, a herald makes an announcement in the heart of the city, then through the streets of kingdom villages on horseback. Everyone dresses in mourning black for the next two weeks.

It hasn't happened in my lifetime, until now.

When I hear news of the Queen, my heart sinks like a stone in a well. My whole body aches in sorrow for Devina.

I still remember, too, what it felt like when my mother died. Like the sun would never rise again. Like the world should just stop its rotation. Like everyone else should be crying all the time, too. Devina must be feeling all that and more. At least the visitors will stop coming to the castle for a few weeks, out of respect. At least, that's the rumor.

Devina's laugh still rings in my memories, like the sound of chimes in the wind. I doubt I'll hear it again anytime soon.

Usually, the kitchen staff are a lively bunch, always joking and laughing; today we're quiet and somber as we prepare the funeral feast.

"She was so young," Maeta sighs. "It just never seems fair."

I nod, halfheartedly knead the dough in front of me.

Maeta pauses. "When you're finished with that, go to the princess. She may need you more than we do right now."

My eyes widen, and I almost embrace Maeta with gratitude. "Thank you," I gush. I knead with renewed vigor, eager to finish my task.

Finally, I take off my apron and throw it on the counter as I dash out the door. It occurs to me, too late, I don't know where Devina's chambers are. No handy map is mounted on the wall, as I learned when I struggled to find the cellars. I could ask someone, but they would scoff if I told them I was looking for the princess.

You? A peasant girl? They would sneer. *Go back to the kitchens where you belong.*

But I'm determined to find her. I'm about to march up to a courtier and ask where Devina's room is when a thought occurs to me.

I turn on my heel and hurry back toward the kitchens, then further into the castle. Twisting and turning through the darkening corridors, I worry I've lost my way entirely when I see a small, huddled form in the shadows, in an all-too-familiar spot.

I almost smile, even though she looks so sad. I sit beside her on the floor, our shoulders barely touching. She doesn't move or speak. I don't either. I just hug my knees and wait.

After a long while, she leans a little, so her head rests on my shoulder. I let her. More time passes. I stroke her hair sometimes, but otherwise, we just sit.

"How did you know I'd be here?"

Her small voice in the silence startles me. "I just had a feeling."

She lifts her head from my shoulder and makes a face. I feel stiff and cramped after sitting against the cold, hard stone for so long; I imagine she's been here even longer and must feel worse. She moves her head from side to side, stretching a little before reaching a hand to rub her neck.

"I didn't think..." she says.

I swallow hard and nod. I understand completely.

"I thought I had more time," her voice trembles. She massages the palm of her hand with her thumb. "She looked fine. I thought... I thought maybe it wasn't serious..."

"There's no way you could have known."

She shakes her head. "I've been so focused on myself and how *I'm* feeling, or not feeling. How long had she been ill? I should have seen the signs sooner."

"Even if she had been sick for a while, I'm sure she didn't want to worry you. She probably hid how she was feeling for as long as she could."

"Then why can't I?" Devina suddenly struggles to her feet.

"Why can't I hide how I'm feeling?" She continues, her face contorted in sudden anger. "Why can't I just put on a brave face and a smile and suffer through it? Why can't I pretend to be okay, so no one has to worry?" She slaps the wall with the palm of her hand, then with the other hand, beats at it with her fists. "W-why did this happen to her and not me? Why can't... Why..."

She dissolves into tears hiding her face in her hands. Her sobs grow to wails as she crumples to the floor, her whole body trembling. I pull her close to me, but she pulls away.

"Devina," I whisper after a long time. Her shoulders tense, and she slowly turns.

"You're still here?" she whispers.

"I'm not going anywhere, Devina. Not unless you want me to."

She considers it, then shakes her head.

"Well, okay. Then let me tell you a story." She takes my hand, and I let her.

"When my mother died, I was in the room with her. I broke a chair. One my father had made, hand-carved. I took it in both hands and swung it against the wall. Then I took a vase, one of our only valuables, and I broke that, too."

Devina squeezes my hand the tiniest amount. I squeeze back.

"My father was so angry," I continue. "He yelled and screamed at me. He apologized later; he was just emotional, too. But when he was yelling, I didn't feel anything. I wasn't apologetic. I wasn't embarrassed. I wasn't fearful, or sad. I just—wasn't anything at all."

"How long did you feel that way?" Devina whispers.

"A few weeks," I say. "It was like I was hollow. I didn't laugh, or smile, or tell stories, or play with the other kids. I sat in my bed and stared at the wall or slept. That was it."

"You felt... how I do?"

I nod. "I think everyone has, Devina, at some point or another. Most of us have felt empty and alone. For some reason, you've just been feeling it for a long time. But you can't be the only one."

She looks uncertain. "Maybe..."

"Maybe no one in the castle has felt that way, but others out there have. Or maybe someone has and is too ashamed to admit it. Don't you think that's possible?"

She looks at me searchingly and then nods the tiniest bit. "It's possible."

"I felt happy again eventually." I take her other hand in mine. "It was long and hard, but I did. And I know you were feeling awful before your mother, but... you'll feel happy again too, eventually. I know it."

Devina swallows. "Will you stay with me until I do?"

I nod. "And beyond."

It happens before I can process it. The princess leans in and presses her soft lips to my cheek. When she pulls away, blushing, I realize I must be bright red, too. We look at each other, wide-eyed, and then burst into giggles.

"You look like a tomato," Devina chuckles.

"Yeah, well, you look like a beet," I retort.

"Beets are purple!" she swats at me playfully.

"Reddish-purple!" I counter.

Hand in hand, we walk back to the kitchens. Every now and then, Devina looks at me sideways and her eyes seem to smile. I think my heart could burst with happiness.

We stop outside the door to the kitchens, and Devina pulls me into her arms. "Thank you," she whispers.

"No, thank *you*," I say.

"For what?"

"For being friends with a peasant girl."

She pulls away and shakes her head. "You're so much more than that."

"More than a friend, or more than a peasant girl?"

Her lips curl slightly, and my heart dances. "Both," she says.

Before I can ask what that means, she says, "I need to go speak with my father."

"Why?"

"Follow me," she insists. She takes me by the arm, leading me away with more excitement than I expected.

9

DEVINA

I don't know how she does it.

The night after my mother died, I sat and stared at the stars beyond my window. It didn't seem fair they got to shine, that the moon still got to rise. I wanted everything to stop, to have everything feel my pain.

I couldn't stand staying in my room anymore, so I fled to my usual hiding spot. I don't know how long I had been there when Yasmin found me. At first, I wanted to send her away—I wanted to keep my grief locked inside me like a storm in a snow globe.

But when I fell apart, slamming my hands against the walls, letting my fury out like huge thunderclaps, she stayed. When I wept, she stayed. She could have sought shelter from the rain, from me, but she stayed in the worst of my storm.

And, most miraculously of all, she made me feel better. My heart, as heavy as it was—as heavy as it still is—felt buoyed by Yasmin's friendship, by her love.

Now, I run down the corridors with Yasmin in tow and nearly run headfirst into someone.

"Esme!" I cry.

She curtsies politely. "Your Highness. Are you alright?"

"I'm looking for my father," I pant between gulps of air. "Do you know where he is?"

"He's in the throne room," Esme frowns, her gaze drifting to Yasmin, "but he asked not to be disturbed."

Before she can stop me, I take off, dragging Yasmin along. The doors to the throne room tower over me. They used to make me feel small, little, but now, they feel inconsequential.

"Wait here," I whisper to Yasmin. Confusion swims in her eyes. "I'll just be a moment." I nod to the guards who oblige my request, pulling the doors open. I take a deep breath, hold my head high, and step inside.

My father looks up and in an instant, my joy turns to ask in my mouth. My limbs feel heavier, and my heart sinks at the sight of the empty throne beside him. I bow my head, confidence waning and my thoughts muddied.

"Devina?" his voice is rough, hoarse. The way the mine sounds after crying. I wonder if he's been sitting here in the dark, alone.

"Father," I take a step toward him, sinking into a curtsy, but he waves a hand.

"Don't bother with that nonsense," he says, referring to my genuflection. "It doesn't matter now."

He's right.

"Are you… are you alright?"

He shoots me a hollow smile, but it doesn't reach his eyes. "Of course I am, my dear," he says. But when I say nothing in response, his expression darkens, and he shakes his head. "To be honest, I'm sad. I'm very sad."

To see my too-strong, stoic father, the King of our nation, confess his pain makes me feel less alone.

"I am, too," I take his big hand in mine. He presses his lips to my knuckles.

"I'm sorry, Devina," he whispers. I think he's talking about Mother, and I open my mouth to reply, but he continues, "I'm sorry I didn't understand."

My brows furrow in confusion. "Understand what?"

"You," he said. "I should have listened, but I was so desperate for you to feel better that I fear I made things worse."

All I can do is stare as I take in his words. My father smiles grimly. "Too little, too late, I know," he drops my hand. "But your mother spoke to me before she…" He trails off. "She wanted you to know we were *both* sorry. That we love you. And that, even if you cried every day for the rest of our lives, you're still our perfect daughter."

My throat is thick with unshed tears and words I can't articulate. Instead, I simply nod. "Thank you."

"Now," he says, some of the usual bravado returning to his voice, "what is it you came here for, my dear?"

This is it, Devina, I say to myself. *This is when you tell him.* But the words are stuck in my throat, and I can't figure out how to get them out.

Then I see her. The doors open slowly and Yasmin pokes her head around the corner, unsure. My nerves melt away and I go to her, take her by the hand, and approach my father once more.

"Father, this is Yasmin." And for the first time in over a year, I smile.

Torina Kingsley has always dreamed of becoming a published writer. By the time high school came around, her mind was swirling with tales ready to be told. She finds inspiration for her stories from viewing things from a different perspective, including her most recent book *The King's Decree*, a chapter book that is a spin on the well-known Russian folktale, *The Princess Who Never Laughed*.

Kingsley believes that a great story needs to be relatable and completely captivating, and that it needs to drop the reader into a whole new world. She hopes that her young readers are made to think by her stories. For instance, Kingsley has seen that, although very few children's books reflect characters afflicted with depression and anxiety, it's something that kids and teens deal with every day, and she wanted to share that in her story. It is also important to Kingsley that characters, such as the princess in her chapter book, aren't just pale, blond stereotypes, but diverse characters who can fall in love with anyone, not just those who one might expect. As an author of Hispanic heritage, representing a diverse audience in her books is meaningful to her.

When she isn't writing thought-provoking and socially conscious young adult stories, Kingsley teaches music and loves working with her students. She lives with her husband and two rescue dogs in the Chicago area where she enjoys reading and spending time with her family.